Jessica S   of Art and Design.
In 1980 she   a travelling puppet company
using colourful   accompaniment and a storyteller.
Her books for Frances Linc   t and funny as her puppet shows.
They include *Rama and the Demo*   *Geese* written by Alison Lurie,
No Dinner!, *In the Dark Dark Wood*, *M   and the Giant Cúchulainn*,
The Famous Adventure of the Bird Brained Hen, *The Little Little House*
and *Sausages*. Jessica lives in North London.

First published in Great Britain in 1995 by
Frances Lincoln Children's Books, 4 Torriano Mews,
Torriano Avenue, London NW5 2RZ
www.franceslincoln.com

First published in the USA in 1995
Distributed in the USA by Publishers Group West

British Library Cataloguing in Publication Data available on request

ISBN 10: 1-84507-506-4
ISBN 13: 978-1-84507-506-4

The illustrations are collage

Set in Plantin

Printed in China

11 13 15 17 19 18 16 14 12

THE LEOPARD'S DRUM

With thanks to Amoafi Kwapong and Peter Sarpong

An Asante tale from West Africa

THE LEOPARD'S DRUM

Jessica Souhami

F

FRANCES LINCOLN
CHILDREN'S BOOKS

Osebo, the leopard, was fierce, proud, and boastful.

He made a huge drum and he played it every day.

Animals came from near and far to see it.

It was a magnificent drum, the best they had ever seen.

They all wished it belonged to them.

Even Nyame, the Sky-God, wanted it.

"Osebo," he said, "that's a wonderful drum.

I should have a drum like that. Will you give me your drum?"

"No," said Osebo.

"Will you lend me your drum?"

"No!" said Osebo.

"Will you let me try your drum?"

But Osebo said, "NO!"

"You should respect me, Osebo. I am the Sky-God. Animals of the forest, whoever brings me that drum will get a big reward."

And Nyame disappeared.

Next day Onini, the python, went to get the drum.

"Looking for me, Onini?"
"Oh, er – no, Osebo…
just looking at your fine drum,
your huge drum,
your magnificent drum…
Good-day, Osebo."

Next day Esono, the elephant, went to get the drum.

"Looking for me, Esono?"
"Oh, er – no, Osebo.
Just admiring your fine drum,
your huge drum,
your **magnificent** drum, Osebo.
Goodbye, Osebo."

The next day,
something strange
moved slowly through
the forest.

The animals were puzzled.
Some were frightened.
  "What is it?" they whispered.
  "Whoever can it be?"

It was Asroboa, the monkey,
going to get the drum.
He hoped Osebo wouldn't see him
behind the mask.

"Looking for me, Asroboa?"
"Ohhh no, Osebo.
Just looking…fine…huge…
mag…ni…fi…cen…t…"

Last of all Achi-cheri, the tortoise,
went to get Osebo's drum.

"You haven't got a chance,"
the other animals said, "not a titchy little,
weedy little creature like you!"

It was true, the tortoise was very small, and in those days her shell was quite soft. She had to watch out that careless animals didn't squash her flat.

"Well, I'm going to try anyway," she said.

"Looking for me, Achi-cheri?"

"Not really, Osebo. I was just looking at this drum."

"Don't you think it's a fine, huge, magnificent drum, Achi-cheri?"

"Well, it's all right, I suppose, for a middle-sized kind of drum, Osebo."

"**Middle-sized?** You ridiculous creature, don't you know this is the biggest, the best drum in the forest?"

"Well," said Achi-cheri, "I've heard that Nyame's got a bigger drum."

"What!" said Osebo.

"Oh yes. It's so big, he can climb right inside it and not one bit of him sticks out."

"Well, I can climb right inside mine," said Osebo. "Just watch."

Osebo began to squeeze himself into the drum.

"Am I inside, Achi-cheri?"

"No, not nearly, Osebo."

"Now, Achi-cheri?"

"No, not quite, Osebo."

"Now, Achi-cheri?"

"Yes, Osebo, now you're inside. But you can't get out!"
And Achi-cheri sealed the drum with a large cooking pot.

"Now I'm going to take you to the Sky-God."

Slowly, Achi-cheri pushed the enormous drum with the heavy
leopard inside it all the way to Nyame.

"Here is Osebo's drum, Nyame. And Osebo is inside."

"Well done!" said Nyame. "No-one else could get the drum. And you have taught that boastful leopard a lesson. Let him go now, and decide what you would like as your reward."

Achi-cheri looked round. All the other animals were looking jealous and cross. She thought for a moment.

"Please, Nyame," she said, "most of all I would like a hard shell to protect me from fierce animals."

Nyame laughed and gave her a tough, hard shell.
And Achi-cheri the tortoise still wears it today.